HORATIO VS. THE SIX-TOED Cat

VIRGINIA SMITH

Next Step Books
P.O. Box 79025
West Valley City, UT 84170

Dr. Horatio vs. the Six-Toed Cat
Tales of the Goose Creek B&B
© 2015 by Virginia Smith

Published by Next Step Books, P.O. Box 70271, West Valley
City, Utah 84170, www.nextstepbooks.org

eBook published by Harvest House Publishers, Eugene, OR
97402, www.harvesthousepublishers.com

Print ISBN-13: 978-1-937671-27-3

Chapter One

W" ell, isn't that the durndist thing?" Doctor Horatio Forsythe lowered his glasses from their perch on top of his balding head and settled them on his nose for a closer look. "And they're all like this?"

Julia Belchwater nodded, lifted a squirming kitten from the basket, and handed it to him. "Every one, the poor dears." She placed a chocolate-brown finger beneath a miniature arm and splayed the tiny paws. "Six toes in front and five in the back."

Doc ran a gentle fingertip over the diminutive creature resting in the palm of his hand, noting the soft bones of the spine, the placement of ribs no wider than toothpicks. The kitten raised a wobbly head and voiced a feeble mewl of protest. The new mother, installed in the basket Julia had carried into the Goose Creek Animal Clinic, extended a nose toward her baby and then glanced upward as if to say, "You be careful with him, Doc."

"Don't worry, Momma." Doc returned the kitten to her side. "I won't hurt your little one."

Belinda, a fine-looking blue-black feline and first-time mom, began applying her rough tongue to the protesting newborn as though to remove any residual human scent from the squirming body.

The worry lines between Julia's eyes deepened as she picked up another baby. "Belinda's favorite place to sleep is on top of that big old giant television set George won't let me get rid of, the tight-fisted old miser. You don't think there's microwaves or electrons or something like that soaking into her body and affecting the kitties?"

Doc laughed, partly at her expression and partly at the idea of what Julia would do to poor George if his refusal to upgrade his TV resulted in her beloved cat giving birth to deformed offspring. "These kittens look as healthy as can be."

"But all those toes! It ain't natural. Poor things look like they ought to be in a circus sideshow."

She extended the kitten in her hand as proof. Doc touched each tiny digit, his finger lingering on the sixth. The extra toe on the kitten he'd inspected a minute before had looked like an afterthought, almost a growth tucked between what would normally be the fourth digit and the dewclaw. This one, though, was fully developed, and the dewclaw oversized, giving it the appearance of an opposable thumb.

The baby issued a loud, trumpet-like squeak as if in protest to its lengthy absence from the nest.

"They're not deformed." He rubbed the tiny head and gestured for her to return the kitten to his mother's side. "Belinda has given birth to a litter of polydactyl cats."

The lines on Julia's face deepened even further. "Sounds like some kind of dinosaur."

"Just means they have six toes. It's not common, but it isn't unheard of either. The story goes that Ernest Hemingway received one as a gift from a sea captain, and the genetic trait spread from there." He leaned against the counter in the small examining room and plucked the pen out of his lab coat pocket to fiddle with. "Who's the proud papa?"

"Don't know. Belinda doesn't like to go out." Her features settled into a scowl. "But when she turned up in the family way, George admitted that a couple of times he left the back door propped open while he was working in the yard. Some sneaky tomcat musta come visiting while his back was turned. That sly boots better not come around while I'm on the watch. I'll give him what-for with the business end of a broom."

Judging by her threatening tone, Doc spared a sympathetic thought for the poor feline who was, after all, only doing what came natural for unneutered males.

The door burst open and a diminutive silver-haired woman entered the exam room. Startled, Doc stared at her.

"There you are, Horatio." She turned a smile on his customer. "Hello, Julia."

Julia broke into a wide smile. "Miss Ernie, I haven't seen you in an age. You're looking fit."

Though officially named Ernestine Clemmons Forsythe, the entire town knew this petite powerhouse as Miss Ernie. Everyone except Doc, that is. He called her Mother.

"Thank you." She gave a regal nod. "You too. Red is definitely your color. How's George doing?"

Julia scowled. "Ornery as ever."

"Mother," Doc interrupted, "what are you doing here?"

"I have something I've been meaning to talk to you about."

"Excuse me a minute." With an apologetic glance at Julia, he rounded the exam table and escorted his mother gently but firmly from the room. In the narrow hallway he gave her a stern look. "Mother, I'm working. You can't simply barge in and interrupt an exam."

She waved a dismissive hand toward the closed door. "Julia won't care."

He fought a wave of irritation. "That's not the point."

"Well, if you'd ever come to see me I could talk to you then. But it seems you don't have time for your aging mother." She gave an offended sniff and managed to look frail.

Doc didn't buy it. Mother might be eighty-three, but she was strong as a horse and an expert guilt-inflictor. "I've dropped by several times, but you're either not there or you're conducting a meeting of some sort."

Now she looked peeved, her lips pursed into a tight bow. "The Fall Festival doesn't plan itself, you know. Summer is my busiest time of the year."

He swallowed a frustrated sigh. "I've got to get back to work. Can I come by the house later to discuss whatever it is?"

She gave a prim nod. "I have a meeting at seven. Come before then."

"Fine. Goodbye, Mother."

He pressed a kiss on her cheek and watched her exit through the swinging door to the reception area before returning to work.

Millie Richardson, morning receptionist at the animal clinic, eyed the desk and slid the appointment calendar slightly to the right so it was perfectly centered. Lizzie Forsythe, Doc's wife, served as the clinic's afternoon receptionist, and she was notorious for rearranging anything Millie set in place. Paper clips, notepads, the dog cookie jar—their placement was always slightly different in the morning. Millie had long suspected she did it in order to mark her territory, though that made no sense since hiring a morning receptionist three years ago had been her idea.

The door behind Millie swung open and Miss Ernie swept through. Judging by her sour expression, her conversation didn't go as planned.

"Is everything okay?" Millie asked.

"He *said* he was too busy to talk." The elderly lady aimed a scowl at the wall, beyond which lay exam room one. Then her features softened. "It's not his fault. Everyone is busy these days. I've been meaning to talk to him for several months now, but seems there's never any time."

Millie nodded sympathetically. "Organizing Goose Creek's Fall Festival is quite a job."

"It certainly is," Miss Ernie agreed. Then her eyes

twinkled. "But I've had a tremendous helper this year. Alison is a hard worker, and quite the organizer."

Millie couldn't help preening at the compliment. Her twenty-two-year-old daughter, Alison, volunteered to help with the festival this summer since she had not yet found a job after graduating from college in May. Of course, her father complained loudly that she was spending far too much time doing free work instead of job hunting.

Miss Ernie opened the front door and a fresh fall breeze entered the animal clinic. "I hope you have a good evening, dear."

A secretive smile hovered around the edges of those sharp eyes. Millie's mother-radar went on instant alert. Over breakfast this morning Alison had announced that she wanted to discuss a serious matter with her parents at supper. Had she confided the topic of that discussion to Miss Ernie?

Never one to beat around the bush, Millie took the direct approach. "Do you know what Alison wants to talk with us about?"

Again, that taciturn smile. "Just keep an open mind, darlin'. She's got a good head on her shoulders."

With that unenlightening comment, Miss Ernie made her exit. Millie snatched up the phone and speed-dialed a number.

"Al Richardson," said the familiar, beloved voice of her husband.

"Albert," she hissed. "She told Miss Ernie."

A loud sigh sounded through the receiver, one she recognized as Albert's attempt to exercise patience before speaking. After thirty-two years of marriage there were very few of Albert's moods that she couldn't gauge simply by hearing him breathe.

Remorse struck her. "You're busy. I'm sorry."

A few moments ago she had been irritated when Miss Ernie marched past her desk to interrupt Doc's work, and here she'd done the same thing.

"I'm in the middle of a program, but it's okay." Albert worked as a computer analyst for a corporation in Lexington forty minutes from Goose Creek. "By *she* I assume you mean Alison. What did she tell Miss Ernie?"

"Whatever she's going to tell us tonight."

The answer was delivered in an almost-patient tone. "And why is that important?"

Millie held the phone away from her ear to settle an incredulous stare on it. Honestly! For an intelligent man, Albert could be so obtuse at times. She returned the phone to her ear and explained.

"Because she told her *first*." Millie's cheeks warmed. Speaking the words aloud sounded so...middle-schoolish.

But Albert did understand. "I know you want to be Alison's confidante. You're her mother. But she's always had a special relationship with Miss Ernie. And they've spent so much time together recently it's natural she'd talk about whatever's on her mind."

"I know." Now it was her turn to sigh. "But obviously tonight's announcement is about something important. She seemed so mysterious this morning."

"Well, I hope she's found a job." A grumble sounded in his voice. "She's been out of school for three months. About time that girl started paying her own way."

Millie shook her head, smiling. He could grouse all he wanted, but the whole family knew Alison held a special place in her daddy's heart. The boys—men, she amended, because her married twenty-eight-year-old twins could no longer be called boys—didn't mind. From their first introduction to their tiny sister, they'd fallen in love with her too. She'd instantly become the darling of the family, and had never yielded the position.

In truth, Millie expected the announcement to be about a job. Either that, or perhaps Alison had decided to go to graduate school. She'd mentioned getting her master's degree a few times during her senior year, though Millie hadn't heard any comments about it over the summer.

The clinic door swung open. Doc leaned out to hold it open for Julia, who emerged carrying her basket of newborn kittens.

"Gotta run," she said into the phone. "Love you."

She ended the call and pulled the computer keyboard toward her to key in Julia's receipt.

The surface of Miss Ernie's dining room table could not be seen. Alison, holding a check for one hundred dollars, scanned a profusion of documents. Where were the approved food vendor applications? No doubt some sort of order existed, because when it came to the Goose Creek Fall Festival Miss Ernie was nothing if not organized. But the finer points of the elderly lady's filing system were evident only to her.

She directed a comment toward the kitchen. "I don't see them."

The answer echoed from the other room in a voice infused with equal parts age and Kentucky twang. "Left center. Third pile from the edge."

"Pile?" Regarding the mishmash of paper with a

skeptical eye she muttered under her breath, "There are piles here?"

"Don't be smart, young lady!"

Alison cast a quick glance toward the doorway. Miss Ernie's hearing was as sharp as it had been more than a decade ago when she'd taught Alison's Sunday school class at Woodview Community Church.

Now that she looked closer, Alison detected a messy order amid the chaos. Third from the left? Ah. There it was. She snatched up a disheveled stack of documents and leafed through them until she found the application for Korie's Kettle Korn. Whipping a red Sharpie from its perch on her ear, she wrote *Paid by Check #1327* on the top of the document and shuffled the pile into a semblance of order before returning it to the table. A little straightening wouldn't hurt. She reached for the next stack—

"Don't touch a thing!" The command was issued with a note of authority that instantly reverted Alison to a guilty seven-year-old caught sticking gum under the church pew.

She jerked upright and whipped her hands behind her back. "Yes, ma'am."

Thus chastised, she returned to the kitchen and placed the check in a metal cash box on the counter.

Miss Ernie sat behind another cluttered table like a queen reigning over her castle. Wielding her letter-opener like a scepter, she applied it to an envelope and awarded Alison a smile. "I've been coordinating the festival since before you were a twinkle in your daddy's eye, darlin'. I know the location of every scrap of paper. Food vendors in the dining room. Demonstrations in the study. Arts and crafts in the living room. And children's activities right over there."

She pointed with the letter opener toward the kitchen counter, which to Alison's eye looked even less organized than the mess on the dining table.

"If you say so." She eyed the chaos with doubt.

"I do." The old lady gave a decisive nod as she sliced into another envelope and pulled out another check. "Durnit, he made the deadline. I was hoping he wouldn't."

Alison took the check and noted the return address. "I love Nuts Over Nuts! That man is here every year. The festival wouldn't be the same without his roasted pecans."

"He's an overbearing idiot." The pronouncement, issued through tightly thinned lips, dared her to disagree. "Always demanding to have his booth in the exact center of everything, and then he inflates that ridiculous balloon creature. Whoever heard of an inflatable pecan? It hovers over the festival like a vulture."

"Petey the Pecan?" The mental image of the silly character standing sentinel above a sea of white canopies along either side of Goose Creek's Main Street brought a smile to Alison's face. "He's an icon. A festival without him would be like the Macy's Thanksgiving Day Parade without Snoopy."

"This festival is *not* defined by a giant nut in yellow shorts." Miss Ernie's lips tightened further. "And besides, the man's prices are outrageous and three years ago his pecans were stale. I had several complaints." She sniffed dismissively. "My cinnamon roasted pecans are better than his any old day of the week. I have a secret ingredient."

Alison shook her head and headed for the dining room, check in hand. When her beloved Granny passed away ten years ago, the blow had been almost more than a twelve-year-old could stand. Miss Ernie had known that she needed someone special, a relationship she didn't share with her brothers or parents or anyone else. Quietly and smoothly, she stepped into the gap.

A wave of sadness hit her, so strong her step faltered and she caught herself on the edge of the messy dining room table. How she would miss Miss Ernie when she left. What if the worst happened while she was gone? Though the elderly lady was as strong as anyone and sharper than most, logic dictated that she would not live forever. And Alison had no way of predicting when, or even if, she would return to Goose Creek.

With the Nuts Over Nuts application properly marked *Paid*, she returned to the kitchen in a somber mood.

With one glance at her face, Miss Ernie's round blue eyes softened. "You're doing the right thing."

Alison dropped the check in the cash box. "I know. That doesn't make it easier." With a sigh, she slumped into a kitchen chair. "What if I hate it? I won't be able to just hop in the car and come home. I might not be home for a long time. Things might"—she cast a doleful look across the table at the dear woman— "change while I'm gone."

"Of course things will change. Change is inevitable. That's where progress comes from." Miss Ernie swept the mess of empty envelopes into a trash receptacle resting beside the table. Chair legs scraped across linoleum as she stood. She picked up the can and returned it to its customary place in the corner. "If a person tries to keep things the same, their future will pass right by them. And you, my girl, have a bright future."

Alison couldn't suppress a grin and a jab. "This from the woman who has lived in the same town, the same house even, for over sixty years? Who doesn't own a telephone without a rotary dial?" She warmed to her topic. "Who still percolates coffee on the stove and refuses to use the microwave her son bought her more than a decade ago?"

The old woman folded her arms and pointed a still-pert nose upward. "Cooking with energy waves is unnatural. And perking takes fewer beans, so it's more efficient. Besides, perked coffee tastes better than the colored water people pass off as coffee these days."

A point that Alison could not dispute, since Miss Ernie's coffee really was better than anyone else's. She ought to know, having drank gallons of it while helping with the festival over the past few months. She lifted her mug and drained the last of the fragrant liquid. Yes, definitely better.

"Besides," the lady went on in a contrived peevish tone, "if anyone should be upset by your announcement, it's me. I hoped to turn this over to you next year." She waved a hand to indicate the clutter on the table.

"Oh, Miss Ernie, the town will never let you stop being the Festival Coordinator. You've done it for so long nobody else could begin to fill your shoes."

"Well, they'd better call in Prince Charming and have him get busy." She lifted her pants legs to display a sensible pair of high-top Nike's. "These glass slippers are retiring."

Laughing, Alison left her chair and set her empty mug in the sink. "I hope you get to dance at the ball past midnight. You deserve it."

"Darlin', I haven't seen midnight in five decades."

The twinkles in her eyes faded. "You really are doing the right thing, but I'll miss you. I'll miss our talks, and the way you tell me all your secrets."

"And I'll miss the way you always bail me out of trouble." Alison put her arms around the woman, feeling the sharp bones beneath slightly stooped shoulders. "There's always the telephone. And if you'd learn how to use e-mail we could talk every day."

A chuckle rumbled inside the fragile body. "I just might do that." She straightened and stepped away. "Go on and skedaddle now. You've got a chore ahead of you tonight."

Over the past hour helping Miss Ernie with her festival duties Alison had managed to put tonight's discussion with her parents out of her mind. Now the anxiety she'd banished returned as a pulsing dread in her stomach. Mom would receive the news okay, after the initial shock had worn off. But Daddy?

"Wish me luck." She brushed a goodbye kiss against one wrinkled cheek.

"I don't put much stock in luck." The reply came with a smile. "But I'll say a prayer, and that's better."

Miss Ernie's Cinnamon Roasted Pecans

1 egg white
1½ Tbsp melted Brown Butter (Miss Ernie's secret
   ingredient)
2½ cups pecan halves
½ cup white sugar
¼ tsp salt
1½ tsp cinnamon

Preheat oven to 225 degrees. Spray a rimmed cookie sheet with cooking spray. Whisk egg white until frothy, and then continue whisking as you drizzle in brown butter. Add pecans and mix until evenly coated. In a container with a lid, combine sugar, salt, and cinnamon. Add coated pecans, close the lid, and shake gently until they are evenly coated with sugar mixture. Spread nuts in a single layer on the prepared cookie sheet. Bake for 1 hour, stirring every 15 minutes. Make sure they stay in a single layer. Cool on the cookie sheet.

Brown Butter

In a light colored pan (not dark coated nonstick), melt one stick of butter over low heat. Stir with a spatula while butter comes to a simmer. Continue

stirring constantly while butter bubbles and re-
duces in volume. Butter will begin to brown sud-
denly. **Do _not stop stirring_**. When butter turns a
light golden brown, remove from heat and **_immedi-
ately_** pour into a cool dish to stop the cooking pro-
cess. Butter will continue to brown slightly as it
cools. Store up to two weeks in a sealed container in
the refrigerator. Brown butter has a concentrated,
delicious, nutty flavor that is the perfect ingredient
for many baked treats.

Chapter Two

Fragrant steam rose from the simmering pot to fill Millie's kitchen with the perfectly blended scents of fresh green beans and sweet onions. Planning the menu for this dinner had required a lot of mental energy. Maternal and matrimonial emotions waged an equally strong battle. Alison's manner over breakfast—the worry lines in her normally clear forehead, the way her gaze flickered everywhere except at her mother's face—gnawed at Millie's motherly instincts and practically demanded chicken and rice, Alison's favorite comfort food. On the other hand, the grumble in Albert's voice on the phone this morning and his peevish hope that their daughter's request for a family meeting would include the announcement of a job, stirred Millie's deep-seated peacekeeping instincts. Pot roast with mashed potatoes, gravy, and green beans would go far in soothing his bearish tendencies. But roast beef *and* chicken?

Well, and why not? Anything was permissible in the interest of family harmony.

The kitchen timer beeped at six-fifteen. Millie pulled on a pair of oven mitts and opened the door, leaning back to escape a wave of beef-scented heat that erupted from inside. As she extracted the perfectly browned roast, Alison entered the kitchen.

"Mmm, that smells awesome, Mom." She came to stand behind Millie, rested a hand on her shoulder, and inhaled deeply. "What else are we having?"

Without waiting for an answer, she began lifting lids. When she uncovered the creamy chicken and rice, a smile erupted on her face. "You are the greatest, you know that?"

Millie warmed under her daughter's praise. Mission accomplished. "I try. Would you mash the potatoes while I make the gravy? Your daddy called when he left the office. He should be here in five minutes."

At the mention of her father, the lines returned to Alison's brow and she averted her gaze. "Sure."

Few things could affect Millie like conflict among those she loved. And truly, there had not been many instances in the Richardson household to threaten the peace that ought to exist between family members. Oh, the usual adolescent pranks, of course. A few incidents of teenage angst when the twins were in high school. The worst was when the boys announced their college decisions—David chose to attend the University of Kentucky and Doug, Georgetown. Albert had reacted badly that neither of his sons even considered his beloved Purdue. He prowled around the house for weeks, grumbling like a cranky old dog. The whole thing was ridiculous, in Millie's opinion. Children had their own lives to live.

Still, she had been relieved, and Albert overjoyed, when Alison announced that she would attend her father's alma mater. He hadn't even complained about the high out-of-state tuition, especially when the scholarships began rolling in.

Millie glanced at her daughter rummaging in the refrigerator. "Your father is a little concerned about this discussion."

Alison emerged with cream and butter, kicked the door shut, and headed for the counter. "Is he?"

"I hope whatever you're going to tell us won't upset him too much. He's been having a lot of acid lately. I'm worried about his stomach."

The girl avoided her eyes.

"It's going to upset him, isn't it?"

"It might." A sideways glance flickered toward Millie. "It will probably upset both of you." She picked up the potato masher and applied it with force, crushing potatoes like she had a personal vendetta against them.

Millie watched her a moment. It would be best if she heard the disturbing news before Albert. If she weren't taken by surprise maybe she could temper the blow a bit, ease some of the stress. She opened her mouth, prepared to apply whatever pressure was necessary to pry the news out of her daughter.

At the whirr of the garage door motor, her opportunity for foreknowledge slipped away. Albert entered moments later, his jowls sagging with a heavy scowl. To be honest, her husband's jowls habitually drooped — had since their early twenties. It was a matter of genetics more than anything. His father had worn a constant scowl as well. For the first five years of their marriage Millie was convinced the man hated her. She'd gradually come to realize his stern expression was merely the natural arrangement of a square jaw and heavy features, a trait his son inherited. Unless he was actively smiling, Albert scowled.

His gaze fell on Alison, who did not turn from her work. He glanced at Millie, one eyebrow arched with a question. She answered with a shrug and crossed the floor to give him a proper welcome with a kiss and a firm embrace.

"How was your day?" She asked the same question every day, but routines were important. They provided comfort and a framework for normalcy within which a family could relax.

The answer was always the same. A kiss on her upturned cheek, a quick smile that softened the stern expression, and, "Better now."

Alison finished her attack on the potatoes and, looking only a bit hesitant, turned toward her father. Wiping her hands on a towel as she crossed the room, she kissed his cheek. "Welcome home, Daddy."

The habitual scowl softened with a look that belonged exclusively to their daughter.

Millie gave him a gentle shove. "Go wash up. Supper in five minutes."

By the time he returned, her afternoon's efforts crowded the kitchen table. Her next-door neighbor, Violet, always shook her head over Millie's insistence that they sit at a properly set table for meals. No trays in front of the television, no paper plates or plastic utensils, no servings dished from pans on the stove. Meals were family times, even if most of the family had moved on to families of their own.

Albert surveyed the abundance of food, his eyebrows arched. "It's not Sunday, is it? Can't remember the last time we had roast and gravy on a week night."

Millie settled in the chair her husband slid out for her and smiled her thanks up at him. "Since we're to hear a special announcement tonight, I figured the meal should be special too."

Alison flashed her a grateful smile.

They took their seats and Millie asked, "Whose turn is it?"

"Mine." Alison bowed her head, hands folded in her lap. "Dear Lord, thank you for this awesome meal, and for Mom and Daddy who worked so hard to put it on the table." A short pause, during which the girl gulped. "Please keep our hearts and minds open while we talk, and help us to control our tempers. Amen."

Oh dear. Millie opened her eyes and caught Albert's gaze across the table.

His lips pursed as he smoothed his napkin on his lap. "An interesting way to begin a family meal."

Alison scooped a large helping of chicken and rice onto her plate and flashed a jittery look at each of them in turn. "It seems appropriate tonight."

Millie cleared her throat as she picked up the platter and offered the roast to her husband. "Then perhaps we should wait for the announcement until after we eat. Let's enjoy our meal."

At first she thought Alison would disagree. She bit her lower lip as though trying to hold back an explosion. Finally, she gave a quick nod. "Okay. I guess."

For the next several minutes, the only sounds at the table were the scraping of silverware across plates and the clinking of ice in glasses. Alison fidgeted in her seat, her movements jerky. Not worried, really, but she looked agitated. Jumpy, even. The silence that settled between them felt charged with energy. Why hadn't Millie thought to put on the radio? A little background music would provide a welcome distraction from the thoughts flying around her brain. In fact, maybe she'd do it now. She rested her fork on the edge of her plate and started to stand.

Alison stabbed a piece of chicken, lifted her fork toward her mouth, and then stopped. "I can't hold it in any longer." She set her fork down with a clatter and literally bounced in her chair, grinning. "I'm getting married!"

The pronouncement exploded through her lips like a bomb and sent shock waves around the table. Millie's jaw went slack and she gaped at her daughter, dumbstruck. If Alison told them that she had signed up for a mission to the moon she would not have been more shocked.

"But—but—" She closed her mouth and tried to find a cohesive question amid the chaos in her mind. "But you don't have a boyfriend."

"Yes I do." Alison nodded with energy. "His name is Nicholas Ricardo Provenzano IV and he's the most amazing man I've ever known. And oh, he's so handsome! I met him in Florida." Her eyes shone with a sparkle that had not been there a moment before.

Millie stared at her daughter. She had a boyfriend, and didn't tell her mother?

Albert recovered his voice. "Mozzarello? What kind of name is that?"

"Provenzano," Alison corrected. "It's a family name,

21

and he's already told me we have to promise to name our son Nicholas Ricardo Provenzano V. But that's okay, because I love that name, and we can do so much with it. He goes by Nick, so we can call our baby Nicky, or even Ricky after his middle name." Now that her news was out, Alison seemed to have lost her hesitation. She picked up her fork and continued eating through an endless stream of chatter. "And I know we'll have a boy, because there are only boys in his family for, like, five generations and…"

Millie's mind struggled with a suspicion. Alison had gone to Florida in June, three months ago. The trip with friends from college had been a celebration of receiving her bachelor's degree in English Literature at Purdue. Since her return she'd told Millie many things about the trip, all the sites she'd seen, the sailing excursions she'd taken, and how she'd learned to scuba dive. Not once had she mentioned meeting a boy.

Three months. And they were discussing baby names? Could it be?

Albert put his fork down and leaned across the table to look her straight in the eye. "Are you pregnant?"

Trust her straightforward husband to get right to the point.

"Daddy!" Alison stiffened, clearly outraged. "Of course not. Why would you ask such a thing?"

"It's the obvious conclusion when you just announced that you're marrying a man your parents have never even heard of, much less met. And you've already decided on a name for your baby."

She straightened in the chair, her expression settling into the stubborn one that Millie knew presaged an argument.

Before the girl could reply, Millie spoke in a voice calmer than she felt. "Your father's right, dear. It's unlike you to keep secrets at all, much less about something as important as meeting a man you intend to marry. Why haven't you mentioned Nicholas before?"

Alison didn't reply immediately. She drew a deep breath, her gaze fixed on her plate, while a struggle showed plainly on her face. "Because there are a couple of things you won't like, and I couldn't bear to have you try to talk me out of this."

"Things we won't like?" Beneath the table Millie slipped off her shoe and extended her foot to rest against Albert's leg. Somehow touching him enabled her to draw on his strength. "Things about him, or your plans?"

"Both." She cleared her throat and then looked directly at her father. "Daddy, Nick is from Colombia."

Albert's eyes narrowed. "Okay. What else?"

"He joined the army, and he's being assigned overseas." She bit her lip and rushed on. "It's a good thing, because we'll be near his extended family, some distant cousins and uncles he's never met."

Millie's heart stuttered as her attention snagged on a word. "We?" she managed to choke.

Alison gave a hesitant nod. "We're going to be married before he leaves so I can go with him." A pause, during which she bit down on her lower lip and winced. "In three weeks."

It took a few seconds for the news to register. Even then, Millie thought she must be numb from the shock of learning that her daughter had met a man three months ago and kept their relationship a secret. The news that they planned to marry in three weeks and then leave the country didn't strike her nearly as forcefully as it would have five minutes ago.

"I...see."

Albert's face jerked toward her. "You see? Is that all you have to say?" He looked back at Alison. "Do you want to hear what I have to say? No. Absolutely not. I refuse to allow you to marry some guy I've never met and flee the country."

"I knew you'd say that." Alison tossed her napkin on her plate with a savage gesture. "This is exactly why I didn't want to tell you."

"I'm surprised you bothered." His voice rose, and a flush suffused his face. "Apparently you've made a decision without us. You don't want to face the facts you knew we'd bring up, didn't want to have an adult discussion to consider your options, so you kept it a secret. Why not continue the deception? Why not elope? Leave us a note?"

"I thought about it," Alison snapped. "But I decided you *might* want to come to my wedding. Maybe I was wrong."

Tears stung Millie's eyes. Not see her daughter get married? At the very idea, a dull pain thudded in her chest. "Of course we do," she hurried to say. Albert opened his mouth to protest, but she silenced him with a glance and then turned to Alison. "But *Colombia*?"

"I know." Alison shook her head. "It stinks. But Mom, I love him no matter where he's from."

"How do you know?" Albert demanded. "You just met the guy. And unless I'm wrong, you haven't spent much time getting to know him. You were in Florida, what, a week? And you haven't gone anywhere since you got back. You can't possibly know if you love him or not."

"We've e-mailed and texted constantly. I know eve-rything about Nick, and he knows everything about me." Her features settled into an ornery arrangement that looked very much like her father's. "I'd like your ap-proval, but even if you don't approve, we're getting mar-ried and that's that."

They were both shouting now, and Millie's stomach clenched into tense knots. She loved these two people deeply and fully, and knew they shared a stubborn streak strong enough to topple buildings. And volatile tempers to match. If this conversation continued, things would be said that shouldn't, hurtful things that might cause per-manent harm.

She forced a peaceful tone. "Let's all calm down." Reaching out, she placed a hand on each of their arms. "We won't solve anything by arguing."

"There's nothing to solve." At least Alison spoke at a reasonable volume, though with a hint of steel resolve. "Everything is decided."

"I understand that." Millie squeezed Albert's arm to impart both comfort and warning.

Actually, she was a little concerned about him. His cheeks were purple, and a vein at his temple had swelled until she could see his pulse. No doubt his blood pressure had escalated through the roof. She squeezed again, and watched his efforts to regain control. When the alarming color faded a tad, she turned to their daughter.

"Why don't you tell us about Nicholas?"

Gratitude flooded the girl's face, and a smile stole across her lips. "Oh, Mom, he's wonderful. Really incred-ible. The smartest man I've ever met. And funny too." A girlish giggle heralded the return of the sparkle to her eyes. "He makes the wittiest comments."

This was more like it. Actually, watching Alison as she talked about Nicholas took the edge off of Millie's tension. The girl positively radiated happiness. Her face glowed with an inner elation that Millie had never seen before. Maybe she really did love this man.

"How old is he? And what does he look like?"

"He's twenty-two, exactly my age. Only a few days' difference. And oh, he's so handsome!" She folded her hands beneath her chin and shut her eyes. "His heritage shows. Black hair, dark complexion, eyes so dark you can get lost in them. And his lips…" Bliss settled over her features as she wilted against the chair back and heaved a deep sigh.

Albert looked at Millie, eyebrows drawn together toward a pair of deep lines etched in his brow. After more than three decades years of marriage, they could sometimes communicate without words. She read his thoughts as clearly as if he'd spoken them. *What are you doing? Don't encourage her. We need to stand together on this.*

Millie arched her eyebrows and lowered her chin slightly in return. *Arguing won't solve anything. We'll discuss it later.*

She turned to their daughter. "When will we get to meet him?"

Bright eyes opened. "Next weekend. He's coming to town for the fall festival, and we'll get our marriage license then." Her gaze flickered toward her father. "Mostly he's coming to meet you, of course."

Many times over the years Millie had been proud of Albert, but never more than now. Though she knew the effort it cost him, he managed to speak in a reasonably calm tone. "I look forward to talking with him. Does he speak English?"

Alison cocked her head sideways and gave him a quizzical look. "What an odd question. Of course he does." Then she giggled again. "Actually, his accent is so strong there were a couple of times I didn't understand him. But it's just so *adorable*."

Albert actually rolled his eyes, which Millie didn't think their daughter noticed. Alison picked up her napkin and fork and resumed her dinner, oblivious to the fact that her parents were not eating.

"We really weren't planning on events moving so quickly, but then he received his assignment so we had to make some hasty decisions. It was only last week…"

Millie let Alison's chatter float over her, paying half attention to the details of a hastily-planned civil wedding and hurried conversations during brief phone calls to discuss their plans to set up housekeeping on a foreign military base. She toyed with her food, pushing rice around her plate and digging a tunnel for gravy to flow through her mashed potatoes. Her appetite had disappeared.

Millie feared it might never return.

The ring of the telephone dragged Doc out of a deep sleep. Well, that and Lizzie's hand slapping him repeatedly on the chest.

"Wake up. It might be your mother."

Sleep made her voice low, almost gravely, but certainly didn't affect her strength. Chin stinging from a misplaced blow, Doc rolled away from his wife as he fumbled for the phone. Prying his eyes opened, his sleep-numb brain registered the glaring red numbers on the clock. It must be Mother. Who else would have the nerve to call him at eleven-forty-three at night?

He remembered then that he'd forgotten to stop by her house after work. Durnit!

"'Lo?"

"Doctor Forsythe?" Not Mother. Female, the voice high-pitched and tight.

"Yes, this is Doc Forsythe. Who's calling?"

"It's Pauline Kramer. I'm sorry to call so late, but this is an emergency."

Doc swung his feet to the floor and sat on the edge of the bed. Kramer. Familiar name, but who—

"It's Rosie." A choked sob. "It's her time and—" Another sob. "There's something wrong. Can you come, Doc? Please?"

Now he had it. Rosie, beloved pet of Pauline Kramer, was due to give birth to a litter of kittens. A registered Siamese, this was Rosie's third or fourth litter. Neither she nor her owner were amateurs when it came to labor and delivery. If Pauline said something was wrong, there must really be.

Doc slid his feet into his slippers and stood. "I'll come right over. Where do you live?"

He scribbled the address on a notepad he kept on the nightstand without turning on the light. No sense disturbing Lizzie any more than necessary.

When he emerged from the walk-in closet dressed in jeans and a tee shirt, he found her sitting in the center of the bed.

"Where are you going?" she asked, voice heavy with sleep.

"To help a momma deliver a litter of kittens, hopefully." He leaned across the bed and planted a kiss on her lips. "Go back to sleep."

"'K. Love you, Doc."

She collapsed backward, drawing the comforter up to her chin in the same movement, and was breathing deeply before he left the bedroom.

On the short drive to the Kramer house, Doc spared a fond thought for his slumbering wife. He'd known her since high school, loved her since college, and married her the day after graduating from veterinary school. It was she who gave him the nickname by which everyone except his mother called him. He even thought of himself as Doc.

It took no effort at all to recall their first date, when she planted her hands on her hips, tilted her head, and batted those flirty eyes at him. "If I'm going to be your girlfriend, I need to find another name for you. Horatio is too stuffy. And I can't very well shorten it, can I?"

They'd both laughed at the idea, and had spent a pleasant evening bantering names back and forth. Finally she exclaimed, "You've got a cute nose and big eyes, but your ears a kind of long. You look a little like Bugs Bunny."

"I refuse to answer to Bugs," he'd replied, wondering if he could steal a kiss before the night ended.

"How about Doc?" She flashed an adorable grin. "That way when you call I can ask, 'What's up, Doc?'"

The name had stuck, and spread. Before long everyone called him Doc. And with such a name, what else could he become except a doctor? Given his love for animals, his vocation had practically been decided for him. And he'd gotten a lifetime of kisses too.

Every window blazed with light at the Kramer house. When he pulled into the driveway the front door flew open and an anxious Pauline stood behind the screen, arms folded and hands gripping her forearms.

"Thank you for coming, Doc."

She let him in, closed the door behind him, and led him down a short hallway. From a landing above, two little girls in nightgowns peered anxiously through banisters.

Pauline caught sight of them. "You two go on to bed, now, y'hear? You got school tomorrow and I don't want you falling asleep in class. Doc's here and he'll take care of everything."

As he passed beneath them a childish voice asked, "Are the kitties gonna be okay?"

Never lie about an animal's condition, that was his motto. He aimed a smile upward and avoided a direct answer. "Don't you worry. I'll do my best."

He followed Pauline through the kitchen and into a small utility room.

"I keep her bed in here on account of it's near the hot water heater. In the winter time it stays toasty warm. And the rest of the year on nice days I can open the back door and let a breeze blow through the screen."

Tonight the room felt hot and stuffy, though the temperature outside was mild enough to warrant opening the windows. Rosie's bed, a round overstuffed pet bed, had been lined with towels in preparation for the birth. It rested in a corner of the room next to a washer and dryer. Rosie herself lay inside. When Doc entered she raised her head, looked at him, and then nosed a trio of tiny kittens squirming at her side. The kittens had been cleaned, and Rosie, though obviously still in labor, didn't appear to be in distress.

Doc set his bag on the floor and knelt beside it. Extracting his stethoscope, he placed the rubber earpieces into his ears. "You're doing a good job, Momma." He spoke in a low, soothing tone. "I'm going to listen to your heart. Don't worry, I'm not going to hurt your babies."

Pressing the drum to her side, he glanced at his watch and counted. Two forty, which wasn't bad considering she was still in labor. Respiratory rate of thirty. On the high side, but perfectly normal under the circumstances. With gentle fingers he probed her abdomen, counting five unborn fetuses before Rosie protested.

He pulled the stethoscope from his ears and looked up at Pauline. "She looks fine. Healthy and strong. What made you think she was having problems?"

"Not her. Them." Pauline's hands clutched at her arms, her fingers pressing into the skin. She dipped her head toward the kittens. "Look at them."

He looked. Three perfectly normal-looking newborn kittens. Ugly and alien-like, of course, as they all were until their fur had a chance to fluff up a bit. But nothing—

Then he remembered.

He picked up a kitten and cupped it in the palm of his hand. Rosie stood to stretch her neck and keep an eye on her baby, which sent the other two tumbling.

"It's okay, Momma. I'm not going to hurt your little one."

With a gentle finger he extended a tiny paw and peered closely. Yep. As he suspected. Six toes.

A quick examination of the other two revealed one with only five toes, a completely white kitten that looked like a typical Siamese newborn. The two polydactyl kitties had orangish-yellow fur and hints of the telltale black lines of a common tabby.

"What's wrong with them, Doc?" Tears choked Pauline's voice. "Rosie's never had deformed kittens before."

"There's nothing wrong with them." Doc stood and looked down at the occupants of the cat bed. "They're polydactyl, which simply means they have six toes. They'll probably be perfectly healthy, normal cats."

"Normal?" Disbelief colored her features. "Look at them. They're not normal. They're not even Siamese."

"One is," he pointed out. "My guess is multiple males fathered this litter."

"Impossible." She shook her head. "I supervised the breeding myself. I always do. And the male's bloodlines are clean. He's fathered all of our litters and we've never seen a hint of…" She swallowed. "This."

"Does Rosie ever go outside?"

"Never. She's a pampered indoor cat. The only time she leaves this house is when we bring her to your clinic, and then she's in a crate. She's never even set a paw in the grass."

The scuff of a slipper against linoleum alerted them to a hesitant approach. "Mommy?"

They turned to find one of the girls, dark hair tousled and eyes wide, standing in the doorway.

"Lindy, I told you to go to bed. Don't make me give you a consequence."

"But Mommy, Rosie did go outside."

Pauline's arms unfolded and fell limply to her sides. "What? When?"

Tears flooded the little girl's eyes. "A while ago. It was right after the fourth of July, and you were at work and Daddy was asleep and I went to play with Melissa and I must not have closed the door all the way." Her confession flowed as freely as the rivers of tears that cascaded down her cheeks.

Pauline crossed the floor and put her arms around

her daughter. "It's okay, honey. I'm not angry. Just tell me what happened."

"When I came home and saw the screen door open and Rosie gone, I looked all over. I called and called but she never came." The child's chest heaved. "I thought she ran away and we'd never see her again. But then she came home." She buried her face in her mother's side. "I didn't tell you because I didn't want a consequence."

While Pauline comforted her child, Doc folded his stethoscope and returned it to his medical bag. One mystery solved. But the bigger question still remained unanswered. Where had this prolific polydactyl cat come from? Even more importantly, how was Doc going to find him? If he didn't put a stop to this cat's romantic escapades, the residents of Goose Creek would soon be up to their eyeballs in six-toed kittens.

Chapter Three

Before Millie opened her eyes in the morning, she felt Albert's glare. As expected, they'd both spent a restless night. Her mind refused to release the gazillion worries that Alison's startling announcement produced. Sleep had finally won out sometime after four o'clock.

Albert, on the other hand, had carried his worries into his dreams. All night long he'd tossed and jerked and mumbled, to the point she almost wished she had forced him to take a dose of nighttime cold medicine before bed. Then at least he might have rested. Now both of them would be groggy-eyed today.

She opened her eyes and, sure enough, found herself

the object of her husband's intense stare.

"What if he's a drug dealer?" Albert asked without preamble.

Of all the thoughts that had plagued her throughout the night, that was a new one.

"Don't be silly." She rolled over onto her side to face him, her head sinking into the fluffy pillow. "He's in the army."

"Yes, but *which* army?" Suspicion colored his tone. "Colombia is full of drug cartels and terrorists. They send people to the United States to infiltrate and learn all our secrets. And what was this boy doing in Florida, anyway?"

"Vacationing? Just like Alison?"

"Or setting up drug deals. Do you know what comes out of Colombia, Millie?" He lowered his voice to a whisper. "Cocaine. His bosses probably sent him up here to scout out new customers. In fact, those cousins and uncles Alison mentioned? They're probably all involved."

"Don't be ridiculous." She rolled away from him and got out of bed. "If you're concerned, ask Alison. I'm sure she'll tell you all you anything you want to know. She certainly loves talking about Nicholas."

"I think you should ask her."

She belted her housecoat around her waist. "Why me?"

"Because every time I opened my mouth all evening she got defensive." He plucked at the blanket, expression downcast. "She used to ask my opinion about everything. But since she returned from college she's someone I don't know."

"Our little girl's growing up," she said softly. "It happens."

"I know. I just thought it would be...different." He looked so forlorn her heart hurt for him. "That's why you should talk to her. If she really goes through with this ridiculous plan, I don't want her last memory of me before she leaves to be negative."

Millie knew exactly what he meant. The Alison of last night, full of chatter and excitement about her young man and their plans, wasn't the same young woman they'd packed off to Purdue. She wasn't even the same person who'd left with her friends a week after graduation to go to Florida. This Alison felt like a stranger. A determined, stubborn stranger that Millie didn't want to make cross. Maybe it was a desire to hold on to her baby, or maybe it was Millie's deep need to avoid conflict in the family, but she found herself wanting to sidestep any conversation that may potentially destroy the fragile peace they had finally achieved at the end of supper. A peace that had come only when she and Albert stopped asking questions and kept their mouths shut.

And yet, an uncomfortable question had circled in her restless thoughts all night to return over and over to the forefront. She rounded the bed and perched on the edge of the mattress beside Albert.

"But isn't it our job as parents to stop our children from making mistakes that could destroy their lives?"

"Is it?" He scooted closer to her side and picked up her hand to entwine his fingers with hers. "Or is our job to train them to make their own decisions and live with the results?"

She leaned her head sideways to rest on his shoulder. "Sometimes this parenting stuff is for the birds."

A chuckle rumbled in his chest. "If only it was that easy. Feed 'em a few worms, shove them out of the nest, and watch them fly away."

They sat for a long moment, drawing strength from one another. Of all the things in the world Millie was thankful for, this man was at the top of her list. He could be a grouch at times, and when it came to money he was tighter than bark on a tree. But he was steady, and constant, and he loved her in a way that made her feel like the most special woman on earth.

Maybe Nicholas would turn out to be Alison's Albert.

"I don't think we should say anything else until we meet him." She lifted her head and peered sideways at him. "Who knows? He might be a very nice young man."

His scowl deepened. "Or he might be a terrorist."

"Oh, come on." She shoved his shoulder with hers. "Do you really think Alison would fall for someone like that? She's never brought home a boy we didn't like. We've no reason to think he'll be the first."

Albert looked skeptical. "We have several reasons. He's from Colombia, cocaine capital of the world. He is taking our daughter to a place where terrorists behead Americans. I can't stand him already." His shoulders sagged. "But you're right. We should wait until he gets here and then we'll have a better idea of what we're up against."

She rubbed his arm with her free hand. "It's only a week."

"And then we'll have two weeks after that," he said glumly.

At his words, an uneasy tickle erupted in her stomach. Two weeks to either plan a wedding or talk their headstrong daughter out of the biggest mistake of her life.

Doc sauntered down the sidewalk and nodded a distracted greeting to Mrs. Emerson on the opposite side of the railroad tracks that ran down the middle of Main Street. Goose Creek had been built in the mid-1800s, one of the many towns that had sprouted along the rail lines around that time. Trains still ran through town a couple of times a week, though nowadays they were operated by regional and shortline railroads, the transcontinental ones apparently not interested in an out-of-the way place like Goose Creek, Kentucky.

The sounds of industry echoed down the street, hammers pounding and Jacob Pulliam's voice calling out for someone to bring him a saw. At the south end of the street, a platform was being erected in front of the water tower where, in just under a week, a series of bands would perform during the town's fall festival. Everywhere he looked Mother's hand was evident. Flowerpots overflowed with orange and yellow blossoms. Orange paint lines on the asphalt marked the boundaries of the tents and booths that would line each side of the road. The windows in the buildings he passed sparkled in the morning sunlight, and a few of the crumbling facades even bore signs of fresh paint. Though nothing short of a complete renovation could spruce up some of these structures. Vintage, Lizzie liked to call them. A woman's term for old.

Speaking of renovations. He arrived at the entrance of Cardwell Drugstore. Originally a boardinghouse, this building had housed a series of failed businesses in recent decades until Leonard and Lucy Cardwell bought it and poured their savings into fixing it up. And a fine job they'd done, too. Leonard, a druggist, ran the pharmacy counter in the back, and Lucy presided over a real, old-fashioned soda fountain up front. The residents of Goose Creek rewarded their efforts, and the place soon became a favorite hangout. Everyone in town agreed that the burgers and ice cream sodas at Cardwell's were the best in the state.

Most mornings found at least a half dozen of the town's retired men—Creekers, they called themselves—with their elbows propped on the counter, slurping down coffee and munching whatever delectable treat Lucy had in the pastry case that day.

He pushed open the door, his entry proclaimed by a door hanger with sleigh bells. The handful of Creekers seated at the counter glanced his way.

"Howdy, Doc." Norman Pilkington, a sixty-something Creeker whose face was nearly as rumpled as the shirt beneath his overalls, thumped the empty stool beside him. "Set yerself down right'cheer. Got somewhat to ask ye 'bout."

Lucy placed a steaming mug of coffee in front of Doc, and he smiled his thanks as he slid into place. A moment later she set a plate with a huge iced cinnamon roll beside the mug.

He groaned. "I've already had a healthy breakfast of oatmeal and wheat toast. You're killing me, you know that?"

"Death by cinnamon roll." She presented him with a fork. "You know you can't resist, Doc."

She was right. He snatched the fork, ignored her smirk, and took the first blissful bite. For a moment he wandered in a culinary paradise brimming with a glorious blend of cinnamon and sugar and yeast. Good thing she only made them once in a while. Otherwise he'd be as big as a barn.

Norman twisted sideways on his barstool. "Figured on stopping by your place directly. Got a question fer ye." He glanced over his shoulder, and then leaned close to speak in a low voice. "It ain't possible fer a bobcat and a plain old house cat to...you know." A pair of bushy gray eyebrows that dominated his sallow face waggled suggestively. "Is it?"

Doc nearly choked on his food. He snatched up the mug and gulped a scalding mouthful of coffee. "What in the world would make you ask such a question?"

"Hit's something my missus is on about, on account of her cat. Eulie's all worried Pearl's in the family way. Hit's her own fault if she is, I told her. She shoulda kept a closer eye on that cat. But she swears a bobcat ripped through the winder screen. Says she heard a racket and chased the critter off with a mop handle, but not afore it got to Pearl." He scrubbed at his mouth with a calloused hand. "Thing is, that screen does have a good-sized gash that weren't there afore."

"What makes her think it was a bobcat? Did she see it?"

"Sure she did. Got after him with a mop, didn't she? Said it was a big old thing, bigger than any house cat. Yeller, with stripes. And 'cording to Eulie, hit had yeller eyes." His whisper took on ominous tones. "Evil eyes."

Doc took a second cautious sip of coffee. If he were a betting man, he'd bet good money that Eulie Pilkington had spotted the mysterious six-toed cat.

"Tell Eulie it would be highly unusual for a bobcat to mate with a house cat."

"Dang, Doc!" Blood flooded Norman cheeks and his

head whipped around to check out their nearest neighbors. "Keep yer voice down with that kind of talk. This here's a public place."

Doc hid a smile and lowered his voice in deference to Norman's sensibilities. "Tell her it would be more likely for a bobcat to select Pearl for lunch than for his girlfriend. More than likely Pearl's suitor was a regular old tomcat. Male cats can be pretty determined when it comes to gaining access to a female they've set their sights on. Have her bring Pearl in for a checkup if she's concerned. I'll look her over and make sure she's healthy."

"Thanks, Doc. I'll do it." Norman swiveled toward the counter again, picked up his own coffee mug, and changed the subject with an observation designed to be overheard by everyone. "I hear this year's festival is gonna be the best yet. Yer ma's doin' a fine job, Doc. As usual."

Slicing off another bite of cinnamon roll, Doc voiced a distracted agreement. The Pilkington place was located on the other side of the Goose Creek Park, not far from the house where he'd grown up and Mother still lived. It backed up to several hundred acres of densely wooded land. The perfect place for a feral cat to hide. A feral cat that he had to catch and neuter.

And he had an idea.

Millie wasn't sure she'd just heard her boss correctly. "You want me to ask them what?"

Doc propped himself on the edge of the reception counter. "If they have a cat that's either in season or close. And if so, would they let us borrow her for a day or two."

Yes, that's what she thought he'd said. Just to clarify, "Because we're going to use them as bait to lure a wild tomcat into the clinic.'"

"Exactly." Doc gave a decisive nod. "Stress that we'll take very good care of them and they'll come to no harm. And in exchange, we'll make an appointment to have their cat spayed for free."

Though everyone in town knew Doc's stance on neutering their pets, Millie had never heard him offer to do the procedure for free. She tilted her head and gave him a look out of the corner of her eyes. "Does Lizzie know about this offer?"

He waved a hand, dismissing the question. "Don't worry about it. Just make the calls."

He disappeared through the swinging doors that separated the reception room from the clinic's examination area. Millie stared after him. If she'd wanted a distraction from her thoughts, here was the perfect one. First, she'd need to go through the files and identify all the female feline patients. The information sheet inside each folder would disclose whether or not the cat had been spayed. From there she'd make a list. She began to relax. Millie liked lists. One could accomplish much if one were working from a well-organized list.

She slid open a drawer and extracted a fresh legal pad. Simply holding a pen poised over the first page gave her a feeling of control. Given the number of client files she had to go through and the resulting phone calls she'd have to make, this task would take the better part of a week to complete. A much-needed distraction from her worries about Alison and her engagement to a Colombian drug lord.

Stop it!

She dismissed the thought, determined not to let Albert's gloomy predictions get the better of her.

Chapter Four

I don't know." Alison recorded the numbers from the check from Krafty Kentucky Belles onto a deposit slip. "The conversation ended up okay, but they're acting weird. Mom kept staring at me over breakfast with these moon eyes, and Daddy didn't speak at all."

Miss Ernie sat enthroned before her cluttered kitchen table, wielding her letter opener like a weapon against a diminishing pile of envelopes. She tilted her head to catch Alison in a glance over the top of her purple readers. "What did you expect, dear? A celebration dance? Their only daughter is marrying a man they've never met and then moving away. They wouldn't be normal if they didn't have some reservations."

"Oh, they have reservations all right." Alison's shoulders heaved with a bitter laugh. "They voiced them loud and clear last night. But then they stopped. And this morning they gave me the silent treatment." She set the check aside and leaned across the table. "It was creepy, you know? Like they talked about me behind my back and decided how to approach me."

The older lady erupted in amused laughter. "Well, of course they did." She sobered. "I've known your mother since she was born, and your father for more than twenty years, since they moved back to Goose Creek when your brothers were toddlers. They're good people, Alison. And they love you. Once they see how happy you are with this young man, they'll be happy for you." She straightened and sliced into another envelope. With a downward glance, she heaved a heavy sigh and rolled her eyes toward the ceiling. "Oh, how I detest the maneuverings that go on during the festival. Look at this."

She extended a handwritten letter scrawled on lined paper. Jagged edges still dangled where the page had been ripped from a spiral notebook. Alison took it and read the painfully cramped script.

Dear Organization Committee,

Thank you for approving my application for attendance at the Goose Creek Fall Festival. I will need a place close to a real bathroom. Not one of those disgusting portable toilets you usually put me by. I can't be within a hundred feet of them, as I believe they are a germination ground for all sorts of diseases and I am susceptible because of an undisclosed health condition. Instead, I'd like to request a tent near the cheesesteak vendor, as that is the only festival food I am permitted to eat due to medical reasons.

If necessary, I can produce a doctor's notice, though he charges $15 that I'll expect the festival to pay for.

Sincerely,

Vanetta Abernathy
Owner, Abernathy Hobbycrafts

A smile twitched at Alison's lips. "She can only eat cheesesteak? Really?"

Miss Ernie gave a disgusted grunt. "I can't stand that woman. Always complaining to the other vendors, trying to stir them up against me. The one year I put her where she wanted, she complained that the booth next to her had cheaper prices and that I was trying to sabotage her. Last year she asked to be put next to the funnel cake vendor. As for a doctor's notice, I dare her to produce one." She rose from her chair and crossed to the giant chart that covered one wall in her cozy kitchen. With a black marker, she scrawled *Abernathy* in the slot directly next to the line of port-a-potties at the north end of Main Street. "There. See how she likes that."

"You really have done this too long," Alison commented while the old lady returned to her chair. "You're getting cynical."

"Don't I know it." Round blue eyes twinkled across the table. "What this town needs is new blood and a fresh approach. If only my protégé weren't leaving the country."

Guilt stabbed at Alison's chest. How long would she be gone? She had no idea, and neither did Nick. So many things could change in her absence. She reached across the table with an outstretched hand, and Miss Ernie took it.

"Promise me you'll be here when I come back." Though she tried to filter the pleading from her tone, she heard it anyway.

"I promise no such thing. I'm thinking about moving to Florida after this festival. These old bones don't relish going through another harsh Kentucky winter." Miss Ernie smiled and gave her hand a squeeze. "But I promise to come to your wedding, if I'm invited."

"You know you are."

Alison released her hand and picked up the check. She headed for the living room to find the appropriate application and mark it *Paid*.

"Hey, I haven't seen Jordan in a while," she called toward the kitchen. "Is he doing okay?"

"That rascal?" She returned to the kitchen in time to see Miss Ernie blow a raspberry. "He's around. All I have to do is think about cooking a meal and here he comes." She peered again over the top of her readers and asked sarcastically, "Are you going to invite him to the wedding?"

Alison giggled. "Can't you just see Daddy's face?" Then she sobered. "I'll miss Jordan too. And..." Emotion clogged her throat at the idea of all the people she would miss when she moved away, beginning with the dear soul in front of her.

"Yes, Clara, that's right. Entirely for free."

Millie clicked her pen open and closed while she listened to the woman on the other end of the phone exclaim over Doc's generous gesture.

"Yes, he is a great doctor." She smiled at her boss, who had perched on the corner of her desk to listen to her side of the conversation.

The days before the beginning of the festival had sped by, as Millie had hoped they would. Her mornings stayed busy working on Doc's project. Turned out their feline patients were, for the most part, spayed. Doc had done a good job of teaching most of the pet owners who came to his clinic to act responsibly in that respect. In order to find a few likely candidates, she ended up relying on word of mouth, which was the most effective form of communication in Goose Creek anyway. Pamela Spencer knew Beth Kidwell had a cat, and Beth suggested she call Clara Wyatt since her cat was always having kittens.

"You will?" She gave Doc a thumbs-up. "That's great. Yes, just bring her by the clinic in the morning. We'll keep her over the weekend, and then Doc will perform the procedure on Monday. You can pick her up Monday afternoon. She'll be fine. We'll take good care of her. Thank *you.*"

She replaced the receiver. "That's four." She clicked her pen open and checked the box beside Clara Wyatt's name.

"Excellent." Doc hefted himself off the counter and offered his palm for a high-five, which she provided. "I have a good feeling about this plan. Our polydactyl friend's amorous adventures are about to come to an end."

Millie voiced a question that had niggled at her. "When you do catch him, what are you going to do with him?"

"That depends. If he's friendly, I'll neuter him and try to find him a home. If he's truly feral..." He left the cat's fate dangling ominously and disappeared through the clinic door.

Millie closed her notebook and placed it in the desk. Hopefully the cat would be amiable and sociable. Surely someone would want him. If only Albert weren't allergic to cats, she'd take him herself. After all, the house would be a lonely place after Alison left.

Swallowing a wave of sorrow, she extracted a second notebook from her handbag and opened it to the page with her current To Do list. If her mornings had been satisfyingly busy the past week, her afternoons had been frantically so. Nicholas would arrive late Friday afternoon, just over twenty-four hours from now, and the house was nearly ready for his visit. Everything had been scrubbed and cleaned, even beneath the entertainment center in the den. Oh, how Albert complained when she asked him to move it, but she ignored his grousing. Nicholas might not see beneath the heavy piece of furniture, but *she* would know the carpet there had not been vacuumed since early spring.

Why was she going to all this trouble for, as Albert put it, Alison's Colombian drug lord? The question had taken her a few days to answer in her own mind. Because cleaning was therapeutic. Scrubbing away the old dirt and removing the clutter worked wonders on a person's stress level. And besides, Alison appreciated her efforts.

"You're awesome, Mom," she'd said yesterday when Millie emerged from a sparkling guest bathroom. "Nick is going to love you."

"As long as he loves *you*," she had replied, pasting on a smile that hid her worries.

She glanced down the list. There wasn't much left to do in the way of cleaning. On the next page she examined her menu, which had been the source of much anguish. What does one feed someone from a foreign country? Her chicken enchiladas always got rave reviews from her family, but she didn't dare feed Mexican food to someone from Latin America. His mother's enchiladas probably weren't made with cream of chicken soup.

In the end she'd decided on meatloaf. One couldn't go wrong with a good meatloaf.

The door opened and Lizzie breezed in. "Sorry I'm late. I got held up by a flatbed with a pile of tents blocking Walnut Street."

Millie glanced at the clock. One fifteen. "I hadn't even noticed."

"I'll be so glad when this weekend is over." Lizzie bustled around the reception counter, opened the bottom drawer of the file cabinet, and dropped her purse in. "I know the festival is important for the town, but it certainly is a disruption."

Before Millie even got out of the chair, she began rearranging things on the desk. The paperclips went to the left of the calendar, and the pen holder in their place.

Millie fought a wave of irritation and retrieved her purse. "I'll see you tomorrow."

"Ta ta," Lizzie replied in her sing-song voice while sliding the dog treat jar an inch to the right.

Setting her teeth together, Millie left the clinic.

Chapter Five

"I promise Snowball will be fine, Mrs. Kidwell." Doc placed a reassuring arm around the anxious woman's shoulders. "We're going to take good care of her."

They stood in the clinic's boarding area, a large space off the main hallway beyond the three small exam rooms. A rack of crates in varying sizes were secured to shelves lining two walls, and the fluffy white cat had just been deposited in a large one, the fourth and last feline to arrive for Doc's kitty slumber party.

The middle-aged woman clutched the straps of her purse, her eyes fixed on her pet. "But she's never been away from home overnight. What if she won't eat?"

Judging by Snowball's girth, he didn't think that would be a problem. "I have a lot of experience with finicky felines," he assured the fretful woman. "And later on today we'll see if she wants to make a friend or two."

He gestured toward the mellow calico in the next crate, who had stretched out sphinxlike on a cushion and regarded them with an unblinking green stare.

"Now, you just go along and leave her to me." He turned the woman around and guided her gently from the room. Holding the swinging door open for her to enter the reception area, he asked a conversational question. "Are you planning to attend the festival this weekend?"

"What?" Mrs. Kidwell pulled her gaze from the door to his face. "Oh. Yes. My nephew's bluegrass band is playing tomorrow evening."

"I'll try to stop by for that. I love good bluegrass music."

The first smile he'd seen appeared on her face. "Then maybe you'd better miss their performance. They're not very good."

Laughing, he escorted her past the reception desk and, after more assurances that Snowball would be well cared for, closed the front door behind her. Turning to Millie, he rubbed his hands together.

"Now, let's go catch a tomcat."

Together they returned to the boarding room. The back door opened onto a fenced-in exercise area. They had no dogs at the moment, so he'd installed his four felines in the larger dog cages. He rattled the door knob to satisfy himself that the lock was secure and the deadbolt in place.

"You're kidding, right?" Millie watched with her arms folded. "You think he's going to open a closed door?"

"This is a very determined cat we're talking about." But he grinned to show her he knew he was being overly precautious.

The room had two windows, one on either side of the door, and he cracked one open about eight inches. He'd removed the screen that morning. No sense inviting the tomcat to vandalize his property. From a box in the corner he extracted the contraption he'd made last night. It jangled loudly as he lifted it.

"Give me a hand, would you?"

Millie came forward. "What in the world is that thing?"

"An alarm, of course."

He'd gotten the idea from the bells hanging on the door at Cardwell Drug Store. To a thirty-six-inch wooden rod he had tied long strings, one every half-inch. At the end of each string hung a bell. They were all different sizes, and he'd had to visit every craft store in the nearby city of Lexington to find enough, but they would do the trick.

She jingled a bell "Won't the noise scare him off."

"Not if he's as determined as he's been in the past. You'll find some clips in there." He nodded toward the box while he held his contraption. "Fasten them to the curtain rod, would you?"

The plastic clips he'd dug out of the Christmas stuff stored in the attic. He'd used them to hang lights on the rain gutters last year. Millie stood on a chair and did as instructed, and when the clips were in place, he secured his homemade alarm.

She hopped off the chair and stood back to admire her handiwork.

When she ran a hand across the strings, the resulting jingle filled the room with satisfying volume. He should be able to hear that from any of the exam rooms. And they'd prop open the swinging door that separated the clinic from the reception area so Millie and Lizzie could hear it from the front if he missed it.

"You know, this might actually work." She awarded him a congratulatory smile.

"Of course it will work." He gestured toward the four cats. "What red-blooded Romeo could resist paying a visit to our lovely guests?"

"Speaking of Romeos." Worry lines appeared on Millie's forehead as she glanced at her watch. "Alison's boyfriend is on his way. He'll be here around six."

Though Millie had not said much about this visit, Doc knew she was anxious about it. "Do you need to leave? Our schedule is light today. I'm sure I can handle the morning myself if you have things to do."

"Thanks, but no. Everything's ready. Alison insisted that we eat festival food this evening. She thinks that'll be easier on him than having us stare across the dining room table at him while he chews. We're saving the family dinner for tomorrow night, after he's gotten used to us." Her shoulders heaved with a silent laugh. "She's probably right. Albert can be a bit intimidating."

The sound of the front door opening reached them. Millie glanced at her watch. "There's your ten o'clock appointment."

She hurried from the room. Doc paused in the doorway, looking back at his invention. Now, how long before his polydactyl friend paid a visit?

Exactly ninety-seven minutes.

Doc was in exam room one listening to the heartbeat of Larry Greely's birddog when the sound of bells jingled through the open doorway. He snatched the stethoscope from his ears.

Larry glanced down the hallway. "What was that?"

"Be right back," Doc whispered as he sprinted from the room.

Millie appeared in the hallway, looking toward the boarding room through round eyes. Doc held a finger to his lips as he dashed past. Human voices nearby might spook a feral cat. He raced through the reception area, drawing stares from a woman and child waiting with their yellow lab puppy, and through the front door.

Outside, he tore around the side of the building. He lost precious seconds unlatching the gate—why hadn't he thought to leave it open?—and then forced himself to approach the open window with a quick but cautious step. The sound of his panting roared in his ears. He gulped in a breath and held it, creeping as silently as possible. When he arrived he flattened himself against the building and slowly, slowly, peeked inside.

There! Pacing in front of the crates was a cat. He realized at once why Eulie Pilkington mistook him for a bobcat. This fellow was large and sleek. Plus, his coloring wasn't typical for a tabby. An abundance of black stripes nearly concealed a yellow and orange undercoat. Beautiful markings, really. A fine looking cat.

Doc grasped the center window rail and, with a firm gesture, pulled it down. Bells jingled as the window slammed shut, and the startled cat jumped. He whirled, and Doc found himself staring through the glass into a pair of amber eyes.

I've got you, you sneaky fellow.

The cat wasted no time. With a giant leap, he scurried through the door.

Congratulating himself, Doc trotted around the building and cracked the front door open enough to allow his body to squeeze through.

Inside, he found pandemonium.

An orange and black streak raced through the swinging clinic door, which had been propped open. It careened into Millie's legs and sent her toppling backward into her chair. The door swung wide and Betty the Birddog plowed through, the air ringing with her deep-throated bark and Larry a half-step behind. The cat leapt onto Millie's lap, startling a shout out of her, and springboarded onto the desk. Betty continued her pursuit, thankfully bypassing the stunned receptionist, and with a giant leap landed on the desk. Papers scattered like confetti at New Year's. A pair of panicked amber eyes flew past Doc as the cat vaulted from the countertop into the waiting room. Larry tackled Betty and managed to hook her by the collar, but not before the dog treat jar crashed to the floor and shattered.

In the waiting area, the woman shrieked and the little girl started to cry. Her mother pulled the child onto her lap while the puppy bounded over to investigate the terrified, hissing creature hovering in the corner beneath a chair.

Doc plunged forward to rescue the puppy, who was about to become the unwitting victim of a pair of razor sharp claws. He'd just gotten hold of the dog when the front door opened.

Whirling, he extended a hand toward it and shouted, "No!"

Too late.

The cat, sensing an escape route, dashed from beneath the chair. Before Doc could take more than a step, the creature darted to freedom between the legs of a startled Lizzie.

Thrusting the puppy into the child's arms, Doc raced past his wife and emerged into the sunshine in time to see a blur of orange and black disappear between the buildings across the street.

Chapter Six

Millie recounted the story to Albert over a glass of iced tea at the kitchen table while they waited for Nicholas to arrive.

"I thought Doc was going to hyperventilate." She wiped condensation from her glass with a napkin, chuckling at the memory. "And Lizzie felt terrible, of course, but it wasn't her fault. How could she have known?"

"What's he going to do now?"

"Keep trying, though he's afraid the cat won't return to the clinic no matter how many females we have."

"Probably not." Albert glanced at his watch for the third time in as many minutes. "It's six-forty. If he doesn't get here soon, can we have a snack?"

The question sounded peevish, which tended to happen when Albert's supper was delayed. Fluctuations in his blood sugar affected him more intensely now than in his younger days. For that reason, Millie tried to keep to a strict schedule.

"How about some cheese and crackers?"

"Perfect."

She started to rise, but halted when Alison's shout from the living room reached them.

"He's here! Nick is here!"

Millie and Albert locked gazes across the table. His features underwent a change. The scowl deepened and the corners of his lips tugged downward as though the weight of his jowls was too much to bear.

"Be nice," she cautioned. "Remember to keep an open mind."

"The same to you."

"I'm always nice. Whereas you..." She finished the phrase with a knowing glance.

"I will be my usual charming self," he assured her as he rose.

She rolled her eyes in mock-exasperation. "Heaven help us!"

Giving her the private grin that never failed to charm her, Albert offered his arm. "Shall we go = meet the drug lord, Mrs. Richardson?"

"Stop calling him that." She delivered a reprimand with a tap on his shoulder before tucking her hand into the crook of his elbow. After drawing a fortifying breath, she nodded. "I'm as ready as I'll ever be."

The front door stood open, and through it Millie caught a glimpse of Alison racing across the front lawn. They followed, exiting the house arm-in-arm.

"At least he drives an American car," Albert muttered. "Probably part of his cover."

A nervous giggle threatened, and she clamped her teeth against it. The car was blue, a newer model Ford, though Millie wasn't sure what model because she rarely noticed such things. Instead she watched her daughter race around the bumper, whip open the door, and throw herself into the arms of the man who emerged before he had a chance to fully stand. Their kiss, about which he seemed as enthusiastic as she, definitely went beyond the greeting of friends. It continued the entire time Millie and Albert took to leave the porch and walk at a slow, sedate pace, down the walkway. They came to a stop at the curb and waited for the two to separate.

Albert finally cleared his throat. "Ahem."

Nicholas broke the embrace, though he kept his arm around Alison's waist as he came toward them.

Her attention fully on her beau, Alison voiced the introduction without a glance in their direction. "Mom, Daddy, I'd like you to meet my fiancé, Nicholas Ricardo Provenzano IV. Nick, these are my parents."

The young man took a half-step toward them, right hand extended, and then stopped to whip a baseball cap off his head. Dark hair cropped military-short had grown out just enough to show a hint of a wave.

He took Albert's hand. "It's a pleasure to finally meet you, sir." A deep southern drawl stretched his words out to twice their normal length. Dark eyes framed by thick, black lashes switched from Albert to Millie. "And you too, ma'am. Been lookin' forward to it. Alison's told me all about you."

Millie stared at him. How could this young man be from Colombia? Fresh-faced and eager, he looked like the all-American boy-next-door. In a distant part of her numb brain she recognized that Albert had released the boy's hand, and it was now extended toward her. Dazed, she took it.

"My mama asked me to give you a message the minute we met." An appealing grin unearthed an adorable pair of dimples in his darkly-tanned cheeks. "She's upset on account of not gettin' to come up here and meet y'all, but she had some stuff going on this weekend and couldn't get away. But she told me to tell you she's wantin' to help with the wedding, and she hopes you won't mind if she brings a few gallons of sauce for the supper after."

"Sauce?"

"Marinara." The dimples put in a reappearance. "A secret recipe from all the way back to my daddy's great, great grandma, or some such. My grandma passed on the recipe to Mama on their wedding day, and she's already planning to give it to Alison on ours."

The smile he turned toward Alison held so much love that Millie's heart flip-flopped in her chest.

Beside her, Albert seemed to gather height as he towered above them all. "Wait a minute." The stern note in his voice echoed down the street. He speared Nicholas with an accusatory glare. "You're not South American."

"Uh, no, sir. I'm not." The young man cast a confused glance toward Alison. "Am I s'posed to be?"

"You're supposed to be Colombian." He directed the accusation toward their daughter.

Alison stared at Albert, confused. "What are you talking about? I told you—" She halted. A hand rose to cover her mouth, and a few seconds later she doubled over with laughter.

Millie realized the misunderstanding then. Nicholas's dark hair and eyes, swarthy complexion, full lips and classically-shaped nose. And the family marinara sauce recipe. All part of his family heritage, as Alison had told them.

"You're Italian," she accused.

"Yes ma'am." Obviously confused, he looked from her to Alison, who was laughing uncontrollably. "Or, my grandparents were. I'm American."

Alison recovered a modicum of control. "Daddy, Nicholas isn't from Colombia, South America. He's from *Columbia*, South Carolina."

Her giggle was infectious, and Millie caught it. The two of them surrendered to laughter, while Albert continued to look stern and Nicholas, uncomfortable.

"Do you mean to say you attended the University of South Carolina?" Albert's eyebrows lowered until they appeared to rest on top of his eyelashes. "That you are, in fact, a Gamecock?"

The question sent Millie into a fresh fit of laughter. No wonder Alison had been hesitant to tell her father about this boy. He attended the archrival of Albert's alma mater.

The young man straightened proudly as though answering an interrogation. "Yes sir, I am. Or was. I graduated in May with my bachelor's degree in business administration."

Albert's scowl intensified. "I'm a Purdue man myself."

"Yes I know." One edge of Nicholas's generous lips twitched upward. "But since you're Alison's father, I'm prepared to overlook that."

Through her own mirth, Millie saw a change in Albert's expression. A spark of grudging approval flared in his eyes. He stepped forward and placed a fatherly arm around Nicholas's shoulders.

"Come inside, young man. We don't have much time, and I have a lot of questions."

Millie watched the pair of them head for the house. Alison came up beside her, and Millie slipped her arm around her daughter's waist.

"I like him a lot." What a relief to say that with complete honesty.

Alison hugged her waist. "I knew you would."

Together, they followed their men into the house.

Chapter Seven

The Goose Creek Fall Festival officially kicked off that evening, when the festival coordinator gave her introductory speech to thank all the volunteers who had helped make this year's event "the best in the entire history of the Festival." Doc didn't dare miss that speech, or he'd catch all kinds of grief from Mother.

He stood before the four crates that held his hopes of finally capturing the source of at least three confirmed litters of six-toed kittens, and four more probable ones. And who knew how many barn cats from the farms spread out across the county would deliver polydactyl babies in the coming months?

Lizzie peeked her head through the doorway. "Are you ready, Doc?"

"I guess." He assured himself that the window was shut, his borrowed kitties safe and secure. "I might grab a sleeping bag and spend the night here."

His wife gave him an understanding look. "He probably won't come back, not after the scare he got today."

"He might." A long shot, yes, but Doc couldn't give up his plan. He didn't have another one.

They left the Animal Clinic and bypassed their cars in the parking lot. The sun wouldn't set for another hour or so, and the temperature promised to be mild this evening. A short walk wouldn't hurt them, and might help lift some of the gloom that had settled on him after the polydactyl cat's dash to freedom.

Band music reached them. The county high school jazz band always took the stage first, a place of honor which was theirs by virtue of being local, not because of talent. Doc quickened his pace. When they finished playing Mother would deliver her speech, and he'd better be on the front row of onlookers.

Lizzie took his hand as they turned onto Walnut Street. "Your mother plans to announce her retirement as coordinator this evening."

"She says that every year."

"This time she's serious. I think it's a good decision if she goes through with it. She's not getting any younger, you know."

"Mother's healthier than a horse. She'll probably outlive us both."

Just before they approached the corner of Walnut and Main something caught Doc's eye. Was he seeing things? He stopped, pulling Lizzie to a halt, and peered through squinted eyes.

Lizzie gave him a quizzical look. "What's the ma—"

"Shh."

With a nod, he directed her attention toward the cat, who had found a wide window ledge to rest and soak up the last rays of the setting sun. A huge cat with a dark yellow and orange undercoat and black tabby markings.

It was his escapee. It *had* to be.

The cat caught sight of them, and Doc froze. The cat fixed an amber gaze on him and blinked. He did not move, apparently dismissing them as a threat.

"Hello, my fine fellow." Doc pitched his voice low. "I've looked forward to meeting you."

The cat responded with a quiet *meow*. No bunching of muscles preparatory to fleeing. No movement other than the flick of his tail.

Encouraged, Doc took a cautious step toward him. "Don't go anywhere, buddy. I'm not going to hurt you. I'd just like to examine your paws, if you don't mind."

Those amber eyes watched him, unconcerned. With a third step, Doc was close enough to touch the animal. This creature did not display any of the behavior typical of feral cats. Up close, Doc could see that he appeared to be well-fed and mellow. Unfortunately, his paws were folded beneath him.

"Would you let me pet you, boy?" He extended a hand, which the cat watched, seemingly indifferent. With the first touch of Doc's fingers, he lifted his head and arched his back, inviting the caress to continue down the length of his spine and all the way to the tip of his tail.

"You like that, don't you?" Doc obliged several times, until he heard the telltale rumble of the cat's purr. Only then did he attempt to pick him up.

When he had the animal tucked securely in his arms, he turned a grin on Lizzie. "I got him."

She approached, stretched out a hand and, when the cat nosed it, ran her fingers down his back. "He's so soft and friendly. Are you sure this is the right one?"

Doc shifted the cat's weight so he could get hold of a front paw. Sure enough, this kitty sported a prominent sixth digit. Not only that, but a quick examination revealed an extra toe on each of his rear paws as well.

"This is our Romeo, all right." He continued to pet the cat and marveled at the way his stress melted away at the feel of its rumbling purr.

"He's obviously tame. Probably someone's pet. How are we going to find his owners?"

"Put up signs, maybe? A notice in the paper?"

The band music stopped. They exchanged a startled glance.

"We'd better hurry." Lizzie didn't wait, but plunged forward and bustled her way past the booths and white tents that lined Main Street.

Doc would have preferred to return to the clinic and install this elusive tomcat in one of the crates, but there was no time. He tightened his hold and followed his wife.

By the time he arrived at the far end of Main Street, Mother had already taken the stage. Her familiar voice rang out across a sea of listeners, thanking everyone for coming out to kick off the festival. He arrived at the stage and joined those standing to one side, since the chairs facing the podium were all occupied. With many excuse-me's and pardon-me's and the occasional application of an elbow, he pushed his way to the front of the crowd. There. If Mother looked this way, she'd see him.

The heavy regard of a pair of eyes drew his attention

toward the crowd. Seated in the middle, Julia Belchwater had a stare fixed on him. She mouthed a question, *Is that the papa?* Doc nodded, and her expression turned sour. He hugged the tomcat closer to his chest, determined to shield him from protective cat owners.

Wearing her best dark blue dress and with every lock of gray hair in place, Mother stood before a microphone stand that had been lowered to accommodate her height. "The Goose Creek Fall Festival would not be possible without the efforts of everyone in town. Thank you to everyone who helped. To Jacob Pulliam and his crew for overseeing all the construction."

She paused to let Jacob enjoy a round of applause.

"To Little Norm for hauling the tents and setting them up."

More applause while Little Norm, who was by no means a small man, took a bow.

"And this year I've had the best assistant any coordinator could have asked for in Alison Richardson." Mother's gaze scanned the crowd. "Alison, where are you?"

In the second row of seats, Alison stood and waved a hand toward the crowd.

"Oh!" A grin lit Mother's face. "And there's Alison's beau, who came a long way to join us for the festival. Welcome, young man. Everyone say hello to Nick."

The startled-looking man seated between Alison and Millie gave a shy nod. Doc examined him from the distance of a few yards. So this was the surprise fiancé. Funny. He didn't look foreign. At least Millie's smile seemed genuine, and even from here he could see that she'd lost the anxious expression she'd worn all week. Even Al was smiling and appeared to be at ease.

From the stage, Mother continued. "And of course every business in town has contributed something. Cardwell Drug Store, and the Whistlestop, and—"

Her speech ceased abruptly. Doc looked from the Richardsons toward the stage to find his mother's gaze fixed on him.

"Horatio, what are you doing with Hornblower?"

"Hornblower?" He looked down at the creature in his arms, who was watching the proceedings calmly. "This is *your* cat?"

"No, he's mine." Alison Richardson sidestepped out of the row and approached to lift the cat from his arms. "And his name's not Hornblower." Her lips twisted and she addressed Mother, who had deserted the microphone and come to this side of the stage. "It's Jordan, after Robert Jordan."

"What kind of a name is Jordan for a cat?" Mother shook her head.

"Robert Jordan was the main character in one of Hemingway's best known books." She hugged the cat, who tolerated the affection with remarkable aplomb. "You can't name him after Horatio Hornblower. That book was written by Forester, not Hemingway."

"I don't care who wrote it." Mother waved a hand dismissively. "I like it."

"Obviously," said Lizzy in Doc's ear, her tone heavy with sarcasm.

The young man, who apparently was not from South America, left his seat to join Alison. He stared at the animal in her arms, incredulous. "I can't believe you stole that cat."

"I didn't steal him." Alison hugged the feline again and avoided her fiancé's eyes. "He followed me home."

Nick's eyebrows arched. "From Florida to Kentucky?"

The delighted whispers of the townsfolk alerted them all to the fact that they had become the center of attention.

Doc stepped between the two young people. "I think we should continue this conversation elsewhere. Let's go over to the clinic, shall we?"

"Good idea." Lizzie spread her arms and proceeded to herd them all away from the inquisitive gazes of the townsfolk.

As they left the area, joined by Millie and Al, Doc listened to Mother rush through the fastest festival kick-off speech on record, so that by the time they turned the corner toward the clinic, she had overtaken them in the golf cart she drove around town on festival business. Alison and Nick hopped on, and the trio was waiting in the clinic's parking lot when Doc and the others arrived.

Inside, they all gathered in the waiting room. The cat, Hornblower or Jordan or whatever his name was, fidgeted on Alison's lap while she attempted to calm him by stroking his fur.

With a scowl that Al directed around the room, lingering longest on his daughter, he took control of the conversation. "Alison, tell us what's going on here. Did you steal a cat?"

"No," she said quickly, and then bit her lower lip. "Well, I didn't really steal him. He kind of adopted me."

Beside her, Nick nodded. "She's right about that. We were in Key West and there are all kinds of cats running around the island."

"And chickens and roosters," Alison put in.

His lips twisted as he leveled a disapproving stare on his girlfriend. "But not the six-toed cats. They're confined within a specially built wall at the Hemingway House, and the males are counted every night."

"Which proves that Jordan is not a Hemingway cat," Alison said. "We even asked the custodian if any of their cats were missing, and he said no. Jordan was hanging around the condo where we were staying, and he kind of adopted me. Followed me everywhere."

Millie stroked the restless cat in her daughter's lap. "So he's a stray?"

"I doubt it." Nick gestured toward the animal. "Look at him. He's healthy and friendly. He was probably somebody's pet and I'll bet they miss him." He gave the girl a pointed look, which she avoided.

Doc turned to his mother. "How did you end up with him?"

Mother rose and crossed the room to take the cat from Alison's lap. "Alison gave him to me."

"Temporarily," the girl added.

Mother returned to her seat, clutching the cat. "For an indefinite amount of time," she corrected. "She couldn't keep him at home."

"On account of your allergies, Daddy," the girl put in. "Plus..." She slipped her hand into the young man's and smiled at him. "I knew you'd probably throw a fit about me coming home in love with an army man, and I didn't want to overload you."

Nick softened visibly in the face of her smile. "But, sugar, what if he belongs to somebody? What if you took some little girl's pet?"

The cat hopped off of Mother's lap and bee-lined across the floor to the swinging door that separated the reception area from the clinic. No doubt he was fully aware of the four females confined in crates in the boarding room

"I've called down there a half-dozen times," Alison insisted. "I've checked the newspaper for notices, I've contacted the veterinarians in the lower Florida Keys, and even talked to the vet in charge of the polydactyls at the Hemingway House. Nobody's reported a missing six-toed cat. Dr. Clark down there told me that the polydactyl gene crops up every now and then around the island, not just on the museum property. She said Jordan is probably a distant relative of the Hemingway cats, but she assured me he isn't one of them."

Nick enveloped her hand in both of his. "We can't take him to Italy, sugar. The army won't let us."

Al jerked upright. "Italy?"

"Yes, sir." Nick nodded. "Camp Darby in Tirrenia, Italy."

"You're going to Italy?" Millie's awarded the couple a grin wide enough to display her molars. "Not South America?"

"That's right, ma'am. The base is not too far from Livorno, where my grandparents lived before they came to the states. I've still got cousins there, so we'll have family nearby." He grinned at Alison and squeezed her hand. "My parents are planning to visit after we get settled in. You'll both be welcome too, of course."

Tears sparkled in Millie's eye, and Al looked as relaxed as Doc had ever seen the man. Though glad for them, he needed to resolve the issue at hand.

He cleared his throat. "About that cat."

Mother answered in a voice that brooked no argument. "When the young people return and set up housekeeping in this country, I'll give him back. In the meantime, *Hornblower*," she grinned at Alison, "is staying with me."

By the clinic door Hornblower, or Jordan, or whatever the animal's name was, let out a yowl.

"Then I insist on one thing." Doc strode toward the cat and scooped him up. He stood to his full height and poured every ounce of authority into his voice. "He'll be neutered immediately. This little Lothario may not have free run of the town. We already have enough polydactyl kittens, thank you."

"I was going to ask you to take care of that as soon as the festival was over," Mother said.

Lizzie leaned forward to catch Mother's eye. "I can't believe you've had a cat for, what? Three months? And you never said a word to either of us."

"I've been too busy with the festival to think about anything else." She fixed a stern look on Doc. "If you visited more often you would have seen him."

He ducked his head at the well-deserved reprimand. "Point taken."

"And speaking of the festival." Mother picked up her handbag and stood. "I need to get back and see to the vendors. If I turn my back for an instant that Abernathy woman will try to stage a takeover."

"Go ahead," Doc told them all. "I'll be right there." He secured his grip on the cat in his arms. "First I'm going to make sure this scoundrel is out of harm's way."

Wedding-in-a-Hurry Checklist

- ☐ Reserve church sanctuary - Millie
- ☐ Call Reverend Hollister - Alison
- ☐ Obtain marriage license – Alison and Nicholas
- ☐ Order flowers – Millie
- ☐ Order cake – Alison
- ☐ Call JW (photographer) - Millie
- ☐ Guest list –Millie and Alison
- ☐ Menu – Millie and Shirley
- ☐ Wedding night arrangements – Nicholas
- ☐ Polish silver – Albert

Chapter Eight

When everyone was seated around the breakfast table the next morning, Millie produced her list. She'd stayed up late making copies so everyone would have their own.

Circling the table, she set one on every placemat and then returned to the stove.

Nicholas picked his up. "What's this?"

"A To-Do list." She pressed a paper towel against the bacon to soak up the excess grease before setting the platter on the table. "It'll expand over the next few days, but it's a place to start."

Alison scanned Nick's copy over his shoulder. "We

don't need flowers, Mom. And I can't see paying a lot of money for a big wedding cake when we're only going to have five guests."

"That's why you order the cake from the grocery story bakery. It doesn't have to be tiered. A regular layer cake will do just as well." She cracked another egg into her skillet. "And you're going to have at least twelve guests, which is another reason the courthouse won't be suitable."

"Twelve?" Alison looked at Nick. "I told you she'd do this."

Millie turned, spatula in hand. "You mean you don't want to invite your brothers and their wives to your wedding?"

"Oh." She looked away, chagrinned. "I forgot about them."

"Plus, we'll have to invite Violet because I want her to make those little chicken salad tarts."

"Who's Violet?" asked Nicholas.

"Mom's best friend." Alison caught sight of another item on the list. "Who is JW?"

"Junior Watson."

"Oh, Mother, really?" Alison rolled her eyes. "I am not inviting Junior Watson to my wedding. He'll wear those ripped overalls he always has on, and besides, I barely know the man."

"He's become quite a hand at amateur photography." Millie expertly flipped an egg. "You'll be sorry someday if you don't have pictures of your wedding. You won't find a real photographer at this late date. Besides, he'll probably do it for twenty-five dollars."

"And why are you and Nick's mom planning the menu? Don't I get to help plan my own wedding meal?"

Her lower lip protruded just like when she was a little girl.

Millie's heart twisted, and she pushed back a thousand memories to focus on the moment. "Of course you can, dear. I was just trying to save you from some of the work."

"Wait a minute." Albert looked up from the list, displeasure heavy on his features. "You know I hate polishing silver. The smell of that stuff gets stuck in my nose and it'll haunt me for days."

She slid two eggs, over easy, onto a plate and set it in front of him. "You have to help out some way. You can't expect us to do everything."

"I certainly can. In fact, I do. What's wrong with their original plan? They run down to the courthouse, say their vows, the boy signs his life away, and the whole thing's over without a fuss."

Nicholas stared at him with a touch of alarm. "Sign my life away?"

Albert laid a hand on the young man's shoulders and spoke as though delivering sage advice. "When a man gets married, his life is never his own again. Trust me on this."

"Oh, Daddy, stop it. You'll scare him." Alison wrapped her arms around her beau from behind and gave him a quick hug before returning to the counter to butter the toast. "He's joking, Nick."

Millie turned with another plate of eggs in time to see Albert catch Nicholas's eye and wink. She pursed her lips and delivered an unspoken warning. *Be nice.* Though truth be told, hear heart warmed to see Albert joking with the young man as he would one of their own sons.

"If you really don't want to polish the silver," she told

her husband, "you don't have to. You have another duty, a far more important one."

"That's true." He straightened in his chair and cast a fond glance toward Alison. "I get to walk my daughter down the aisle."

"That's not what I'm talking about." Millie slid the final egg onto her own plate and carried it to the table. "You get to pay for everything."

Having rendered her husband momentarily speechless, she took her seat and bowed her head. It was her turn to pray.

Epilogue

Millie waited on the grass outside the church, Albert at her side. Across the sidewalk, Shirley and Three, as the family called Nicholas's father, stood arm-in-arm. They made quite a group, the twenty-three people who had gathered to see Alison and Nicholas exchange their vows. Not only her sons, Doug and David, and her daughters-in-law, but Albert's niece had driven down from Cincinnati and brought her three children. Seven-year-old Tori had served as an impromptu flower girl, spreading petals hurriedly plucked from the wilting mums in the flowerpots along Main Street.

"It was a beautiful wedding, wasn't it?" she asked Albert.

He squeezed her arm. "It was. You did a great job."

"Thank you. And you looked very nice walking Alison down the aisle." When they passed the front pew where Millie stood, she'd caught the sparkle of tears in his eyes. But to mention that would embarrass him, so she tucked the memory away in her heart.

Tori, standing on the church steps to peer inside, whirled with a grin and shouted, "Here they come!"

Moments later, Alison and Nicholas appeared in the doorway. They paused while Alison gathered the skirts of the elegant white prom dress she and Millie found on the rack at a department store in Lexington. No wedding dress could be more beautiful, nor any bride either. Alison positively radiated joy when she looked into the handsome face of her husband, resplendent in his military dress uniform.

Then the pair disappeared behind a blur of Millie's tears.

They ran down the stairs amid a shower of birdseed thrown by their guests. Laughing and crying at the same time, Millie waved at the couple as they ran to the waiting car. Nicholas sprinted forward and opened the door for his bride, who turned and called to her guests, "We'll see y'all at the house!"

"She already sounds like him," Albert muttered. "Did you hear that southern drawl?"

Millie laughed. "Imagine what she'll sound like when they come back from Italy."

When the newlyweds' car sped away, everyone else headed for their own vehicles. Albert started to leave, but Millie held him back with a pressure on his arm. He turned to her with an unspoken question.

"I just…need a moment." Again, her vision blurred, and she lowered her head lest anyone see.

Albert pressed her hand and told their sons to go ahead. When they stood alone on the church lawn, he placed an arm around her waist.

"Are you going to be okay?"

Swallowing, Millie nodded.

He pulled her close, and she rested her head against his shoulder, breathing in the unique blend of his after-shave, soap, and hair tonic. They were alone now. Truly alone. The last of their little birds had left the nest.

"Our house will never be the same." Her words were muffled against his suit coat.

"What are you talking about, Mildred Richardson?" She heard a teasing tenderness in his voice. "We've been alone for four years, ever since she went to college."

She shook her head. "It's not the same. She was just away temporarily. But we're really alone now. She won't be coming home." A sob threatened to choke her, and she pressed her face harder against the stiff fabric.

Albert hugged her a moment, and then pushed her gently back. "Here now. Dry your eyes. This is the way it's supposed to work. We've done our job. And we've done a good job with all three of our kids. Now it's our turn."

With a mighty sniff, she looked up into his face. "Our turn to do what?"

A wolfish grin appeared on the familiar face. "Chase each other around the house, maybe?"

The answer was so un-Albert-like that she laughed. Trust her husband to say exactly what she needed to hear. When the laughter died, she was left smiling at the man she had loved for more than half her life.

"I hope Alison and Nicholas will be as happy as we have been." She rose on her toes to place a lingering kiss on his cheek. "I love you, Albert."

"It's a good thing," he replied. "I think you're stuck with me."

Laughing, they looped arms and headed toward their car.

About the Author

VIRGINIA SMITH is the bestselling author of twenty-six novels (and counting!), an illustrated children's book, and over fifty articles and short stories. An avid reader with eclectic tastes in fiction, Ginny writes in a variety of styles, from lighthearted relationship stories to breath-snatching suspense. Her books have been finalists in ACFW's Carol Award, the Daphne du Maurier Award of Excellence in Mystery/Suspense, the Maggie Awards, and the National Reader's Choice Awards. Two of her novels, *A Daughter's Legacy* (2011) and *Dangerous Impostor* (2013) received the Holt Medallion Award of Merit.

Ginny enjoys researching her books almost as much as writing them. For *Dr. Horatio vs. the Six-Toed Cat* she frequented the streets of small towns in central Kentucky, hopped down to Key West to visit the Hemmingway House, and became fascinated with polydactyl cats. And she ate tons of cinnamon roasted pecans.

Learn more about Ginny and her books at

www.VirginiaSmith.org.

Ready for more Goose Creek?

Don't miss the first full-length novel in
Virginia Smith's new series,

Tales from the Goose Creek B&B!

Made in the USA
San Bernardino, CA
03 April 2017